THE D[illegible] AL[illegible]EN CAME

THE DAY THE
ALIEN
CAME

THE DAY THE ALIEN CAME

Written by the children of

Castle Primary School, Roundhill Primary School, St Keyna Primary School, St Martin's Garden Primary School, St Mary's Church of England Primary School, St Michael's Junior Church School, Twerton Infant School and Nursery

In collaboration with

Stewart Foster

Illustrated by

Andrew Prescott

1174 2024 St. John's Foundation Celebrating 850 Years

Brown Dog Books

First published 2024

Registered Charity No: 201476.
Registered Office: 4-5 Chapel Court, Bath, BA1 1SQ
www.stjohnsbath.org.uk

Published under licence by Brown Dog Books and
The Self-Publishing Partnership Ltd, 10b Greenway Farm, Bath Rd, Wick, nr. Bath BS30 5RL, UK

www.selfpublishingpartnership.co.uk

ISBN printed book: 978-1-83952-844-6

Written in collaboration with Stewart Foster
Compiled and edited by Lois Foster
Cover and internal design by Andrew Prescott
Illustrations by Andrew Prescott
www.andrewprescott.co.uk

Printed and bound in the UK
This book is printed on FSC® certified paper

MIX
Paper | Supporting responsible forestry
FSC® C013604

Thank you to our headline sponsors who have supported this project

almeda

CURATED PROPERTY

evelyn PARTNERS

THRINGS SOLICITORS

This story has been written by:

Castle Primary School

Yelysei Bandurenko, Mason Bolton-Clarke, Lilie Brooks, Rylea Buckland, Natalie Chan, Wyatt Clarke, Bella Clayfield, Isabelle Coates, Rosie Cook, Millie Davies, Ava Escott, Kaleb Gadsby, Elia Georgieva, Lily Haines, Cassie Hill, Leo Meredith, Evie O'Hanlon, Mirabel Ololade-Odumosu, Tommie Ralph, Alfie Ramage, Anab Stanly, Luca Tanner, Aria Tsang, Daniel Viswasam – Pugazhenthi, Layla Welborn Govey, Jaymee-Leigh Williams-Marks, Sophie, William, Finley Williams, Lydia Russell, Lyla Harwood

Roundhill Primary School

Aaron Saji, Albert Joshcheruvil, Amahrae Pownall, Amelia Higgins, Anna Jobil, Charlie Fry, Daisy Robson, Efron Aneesh, Elsey Tonkin, Elsie Crain, Frederick Cobb, Isabelle Hepworth, Jack Lambert, Jay Messer, Kodi Smith, Lacey Duffy, Lucas Larcombe, Malakai McCabe, Max King, Max Smith, Molly Shearn, Myah Thomas, Olivia Bass, Phoebe Robson, Rhys Powell, Riley Clark, Tyler-Jay Gillard, Yazmin Lock, Yesenia Oakes

St Keyna Primary School

Archie Alvis, Jasper Buck, Ethan Cadman, Shea Cadman, Ray Charters, Ryver Eddolls, Evelyn Flack, Charlie Gerson, Finnley Gibbs-Valentine, Abiona Issac, Louie Jarrett, Charlie Jose, Alain Manoj, Julia Masiewicz, Quade Mealing, Henry Moore, Matilda Oxenham, Rio Parker, Esalinda Reci, Darcie Richards, Rhia Ruddick, Daren Sasi, Shrinika Sil, Fergus Simpson, Isabelle Smart, Beth Tamblin, Sophie Tippett, Evie Verrier-Stunt, Audrey Warren, Esme Weston, Luca Wheeler

St Martin's Garden Primary School

Louis Thompson, Lexi Watts, Jacob Archer Miles, George

Archer Miles, Harry Archer Miles, Luka Jax Harris, Millie Hoskins, Mason Spurrey, Summer Powell, Derric Nigeesh, Alfie James Lake, Maria Ranete, Ruth Nakazwe, Valerian Okokhere, Archie Charlesworth, Idhika Sumesh, Lucy Seale, Leo James Kent, Harmiony Farrington, Conan Packer, Charlie White, Eva Smith, Joe, Samir Chowdhury, Brooke-Lynn Buchan, Harvey Croxon, Cemre Saltik, Michelle Ihayere

St Mary's Church of England Primary School

Kara Beale, Tommy Bridges, Efa Davies, Erinn Davies, Rowan Francis, Lily Gretton, Poppy Hazelton, Faith Johnson, Erin Jones, Luvinder Kaur, Dennis Kynaston, Sebastian Lake, Baylee Morgan, Rudy Phoenix, Kizzy Robinson, Esme Sayer, Phoebe Smith, Nathan Warren, Ava-Rose Westlake

St Michael's Junior Church School

Walid Alasaad, Trianne Bael, Whitney Ball, Danielle Ball-Nicholls, Summer Blake, Macie Brooke, Annalise Gillard, Kaci-Mai Gillum, Blake Griffin, Amaya-Boe Harwood, Freya Hill, Jessica Hill, Danny Isaac-Jones, Raife Isaac-Jones, Isaac Kelly, Eshal Khan, Ollie Lehtonen, Keyan Marchant, Phoebe Nicholls, Lacey-Mae Pile, Rory Reeves, Beau Richardson, Matthew Seal, Andrew Shell, Logan Shreeves, Charlie Smith-Fry, Pippa Straffen, Sonny Vosper, Sebastian Walley, Harley White

Twerton Infant School and Nursery

Shakai Barrow, Sienna Boyes, Charlie Bowen, Poppy Brooke, Tristan Clifford, Hermione Cooper, Teagan-Jayne Cooper-Newman, Ollie Dalziel, Isla Duncan-Clarke, Amber Fenton, Dolly Ford, Scarlet-Rae Hardy-Beecham, Willow Hemms, Olivia Jurca, Yousef Khalaf, Toby Lawrence, Robyn Ludwell, Joden Magano, Amaiya Maslen, Joseph McLoughlin, Ted O'Donnell, Freddie Quick, Elsie Smith-Fry, Jack Snape, Erin Stubbs, Prisha Thananki, Kerry-Anne Tubbs, Grace Wildmane

Contents

Chapter 1

It's the dead of night, the sky an inky-black blanket speckled with stars. And we're staring up at it, thinking about the places we've been and the places we want to go.

We can be any place and anywhere when we look at the stars.

But on this night, we, the children from Bath and Keynsham schools, are focused on only one thing. That speck of light in the distance, that we've been watching for nearly an hour. Getting bigger as it gets closer, closer – closer still.

This is a night we will remember for the rest of our lives.

We will remember it for different reasons and in different ways. We've decided to write it down in this book, so in the future, anyone can pick it up and they won't have to worry about computers crashing, or satellites colliding, because this book and our story will never be erased.

This book is our story about the amazing things we saw and did when Jai, the alien, and his Grampy, crash-landed on Earth. It's a bumpy ride, so hold on tight.

Here we go!

24th May 2024 22.05.
Location: Twerton, Bath. Weather: clear.
What Andrew Shell
(Year Six, St Michael's) saw.

I was in my house at night.
I looked outside my window.
The moon was shining bright,
then something coming towards me caught my eye.
I didn't know what it was.
I said, 'I bet it's a jet,'
but then it was very clear.
The thought of what it was
filled my body with fear.
It was very round
and had a glass dome on top.
It's an alien spaceship!
It slowly floated down.
Particles of dust fell off from above.
It landed on my roof.
Then I realised, my parents were gone.
So many questions filled my head:
Where did they go?
Did they move out?
I went up on the roof.
The spaceship's door opened to show the inside.
I saw a shelf with jars and planets,
and a green figure with huge eyes.

Meanwhile, just up the road from Andrew, Trianne was in her bedroom, when...

As an illuminous glow shone through my tinted-glass window in my bedroom, I glanced over to see a massive circle object hovering creepily on the cracked pavement in front of my suburban house. The time was three a.m. and I hadn't got a blink of sleep. My gut told me something was wrong…

The object kept me awake even longer, as I couldn't sleep because the muffled buzzing was just outside my innocent neighbourhood. It felt like time had stopped. No one was in this universe. Just me. The object had bright lights on the front. It looked like fireflies were superglued on a doughnut-looking metal circle. Well, at least from my angle.

In the corner of my eye, my chill friend Stella's house lit up. I wouldn't have expected her to be awake at this time, but I had a beacon of hope that maybe she saw it too. My brain told me to get some slumber, but my heart said, maybe this is an opportunity to embark on an adventure. My other friends, Lola and Bonnie, are twins, and live together. Surprisingly, they were awake as well.

Suddenly, large prongs from the metal doughnut-looking thing grabbed all the stars that lit up the sky and squished them into one little ball. The prongs just folded back in slowly, the blindingly bright ball with it. A door on the metal doughnut opened like a door on a Lamborghini...

Sightings of the mysterious object weren't just confined to Bath. It could be seen ten miles away. Here's our local reporter, Esme Sayer (Year Four, St Mary's).

24th May 2024 22.14.
Location: Radstock, Bath. Weather: clear.

Sally was sat in her bed looking up at the see-through ceiling. There was a whooshing sound, getting louder. She thought it might be the washing, but why would her mother be doing it at nighttime? Then she noticed it was freezing, and a veil of darkness had coated the land and the stars had disappeared. The thing that was coming was black with outstretched hands, which were rotten yellow. A wave of realisation struck Sally.

It was an alien!

It was getting closer and closer…

Sally ran downstairs – frightened but desperate to tell her mum what she had just seen – but when she reached the bottom, the stars had reappeared. The landscape was beautiful. The obsidian night was swallowed by the fiery orange sun as verdant meadows came back into sight.

Meanwhile, here is an account by Dennis and Ava-Roses of St Mary's we have pieced together.

We were in a cornfield. We saw a lizard person in a flying shiny mossy ancient UFO. It sounded like a plane flying. The air smelt like burnt rubber and gasoline and fire, and the air was more hot. It felt like this was a dream and soon we would wake up.

Tears ran down our faces. The beast pointed at us.

And the world turned dark.

We woke up in a room, not sure where we were, until I saw it. An alien. It was covered in tentacles, head to toe with a slimy substance covering its body. It popped and one-million-billion-trillion more of them came.

Then a sound.
Like holiday music.
Everything is fun.
Smells like candy sweets,
I feel excited and cold.
It feels sandy and squishy.
It's starting to become clear
a spaceship has landed
on our sandy squishy planet.
Partying aliens are having fun.
Green skin and pink hair.
Talking gibberish.
I want them to meet my friends.
I want us to have fun.

And finally, here's a live report Lucy from St Martin's wrote exactly when she saw it.

I see a deep blue sky with ten-million stars shimmering in the moonlight. I am in my bedroom with one of my friends, Melody. I can hear quiet whirring. I also see a colourful spaceship, which belongs to aliens who are going to land on the orange plain, near my house.

Me and Melody use my high-tech telescope to observe the flying ship. Then I take clear photos of the ship and send it to my friends. But Melody says that she can hear my mum coming up the stairs.

We climb into our sleeping bags and practise being asleep. When my mum comes in, she is fooled by us, because we are pretending to be asleep. A few seconds later, I suddenly wake up to loud whirring coming from the plain. Melody points out a few colourful aliens trying to climb into my bedroom.

When the aliens finally climb in, they use my telescope to observe the night sky with us. They make notes on a large clipboard. Their writing isn't English; I can't understand what it means, but we are happy together.

Chapter 2

You know, as you can see, it seems the alien came in different shapes and sizes. That's what Jai, our alien can do – he can shape-shift himself to be in different places at the same time. But Jai isn't that different to us – he has exactly the same feelings and worries. So did you ever stop and consider what it might be like to be Jai, the alien, and his grampy, crash-landing on Earth when they'd only popped out for gentle intergalactic ride?

Now, suddenly, Jai was looking out of his spaceship with hundreds of our eyes looking back at him. And we tried to imagine how he must have felt, landing in Bath, zillions of light-years away from home.

BATH

You Should Meet the Humans

(Pieces we put together by Sophie, William, and Finley Williams, Castle Primary.)

I was on my spaceship with Grampy when we crashed at a trillion miles per hour and hit Earth. As the aircraft hit the ground, Grampy questioned my driving skills. I looked around at the pitch-black sky.

'Where are we, Grampy?' I asked, shaking with fear. I worried about what was outside. We'd never been on Earth before.

We looked around for a blanket and Grampy found one. I leant against a pillow.

'Goodnight,' I whispered.

Me and Grampy fell asleep.

We woke up in the morning to see children all around the aircraft.

'I've been thinking, you should go outside to meet the humans,' Grampy said. 'The engine is broken and there's a piece of Pepsi can stuck in the turbo boosters. We need to fix it so we can get back to Mars.' He opened the door slightly. It was very warm, and a bit blustery. Some dust got in.

'I don't want to leave. It's scary out there!' I cried.

Grampy looked at me, knowing we will have to leave soon. 'You'll be fine, Jai. I promise.' Then he mumbled, 'I think we will be down here for a long time.'

You're Different.

(Cassie H, Castle Primary.)

It is a rainy and foggy night. Drops of water clash against the top of my spaceship. Thousands of people and children stare at me with wide eyes and dropped jaws. It feels unusual to have so much attention on me. There is 'equipment', as my grampy would call it. Long blue tubes with funny-looking stick-like poles leading up to them. There are very large people swinging on a dangly black chair.

It's odd to see these strange things. I am used to bumpy floors and purple trees with hanging bright-red berries.

It feels like my every move is being watched. I cannot get a moment of feeling alone. What if they bully me? I am much smaller, dumber and different to them. They could be judging everything I do at this very moment. I have never been surrounded by this much of a crowd.

I feel the breeze coming through the small crack in my window. I turn around to look at my grampy.

'Why are they looking at me? Are they judging me?' I say.

He walks up to me. 'They're not judging you, Jai. You're different.'

He reassures me. I turn back around and wipe away the drops of rain slowly dripping down the window. I hope they don't find me weird. I know I'm an alien, but I have feelings too.

Don't Worry
(Lydia Russell, Castle Primary.)

The racket was finally over. I had landed.

Luckily, I managed to get some sleep last night, although now I can't, because there is this blinding source of light. I ask Grampy what it is (he has more knowledge of this particular place called Earth). He says it is a star that goes by the name of 'the Sun'.

I don't want to go outside. What if everybody makes fun of me? What if everybody thinks I'm weird? I already feel like I don't belong.

My planet is nothing like this!

My planet has shelter, but not buildings, and in this planet, you can get in trouble for trespassing. On my planet, you can sleep somewhere one night, then sleep somewhere else the next. Grampy told me not to worry, but if you have an alien Grampy, you can relate when I say…

If someone tells you not to worry,

it doesn't make everything okay.

Eventually, I decide to go out and give it a try in the real world.

Before I leave, Grampy gives me my favourite meal (fish fingers glazed with mayonnaise and gravy, with a side of tuna. Seriously, you should try it!)

Opening the Door
(Two pieces we put together by Lily Haines and Bella Clayfield, Castle Primary.)

I stare at the starry night sky around in the comfort of my ship and holding my teddy bear close to my chest, dreading what will happen if I go out there.

I've never been to Earth before, I think to myself. The controls are still broken from the crash.

I can't stop thinking about the crash.

I walk up to the door.

I look at the button that opens the door and I press it.

As I say goodbye to Grampy, he calls out my name.

'Jai! Remember to be safe!' he shouts.

I nod and take my first step outside.

There's a bright light shining on everyone. It is hot, and every time I look it hurts all of my eyes, so I look away. I realise there are lots of human beings. One of them walks up to me and starts talking.

'Hello… My name is Andrew,' they say.

'Oh, hi! My name is Jai,' I say, waving to them.

'Would you like to go to an amusement park with me?' the Andrew human says. He grabs my hand.

'Sure, why not? Let's go.' I take his hand and we walk to the amusement park.

When we arrive, I run straight to the cotton candy place.

'Ooh, what's this?' I shout to him.

‘It’s cotton candy.’ He walks over to the man and buys some for us.

I pop some in my mouth and it tastes so good! Andrew looks at me and laughs.

TOOTHPASTE

Jelliton
(Lyla Harwood, Castle Primary.)

Crash!

We landed.

I was very tired. It was a pitch-black night. We had travelled from Pluto to… Earth, I think it was? Me and Grampy had gone to sleep as it was a stiff ride in the spaceship.

Earth looked a lot dirtier than my planet. We awoke from the bright-yellow circle thing. Grampy decided to come as I didn't really know where I was going! We saw many different humans.

'Grampy! I'm so hungry!' I exclaimed.

Grampy giggled. I looked at him seriously.

'Oh, Jai. Let's find you a place to eat!' Grampy said happily.

We found my favourite food in something called a 'local corner shop'. I picked up some raw fish and toothpaste! Grampy got the same as me.

We walked outside and sat on a brown wet bench – though it didn't matter, as I am made out of Jelliton! Haha, I know, I'm funny. Do you think I'm funny? Okay, okay, I'm sorry. Let's carry on!

So, anyway, I made some human friends. They are okay… I guess! They are always mean to other people and they encourage me to do it, but I say… NO!

Twerton Infants

The alien is landing on a planet and is surrounded by stars. Prisha.

He's a black alien going to a funeral. Joseph.

My alien has six eyes. Tristan.

Two robots are trying to kill the aliens, but the aliens are fighting back. Charlie.

The alien was in the ocean. It has a controller with a button, which it pressed to go to Bath. Amaiya.

She was stuck on Earth with her babies and the babies are saying, 'What is happening?' The alien came down to get them. Robyn.

My alien has no mouth, but it growls and grumbles. Ollie.

Two aliens are travelling in their jet to Bath. They are going to land on the concrete. They will look for people and eat them. Kerry-Anne.

It's a Queen alien. She has lots and lots of arms and legs. She uses them to pick up and grab things. Sienna.

The alien is jumping because he wants to be really tall. Dolly.

And now here are three poems about the day Jai arrived.

The Day the Aliens Came

Reactive Poem, written together by Faith and Rudy (St Mary's)

On the day the aliens came,
I was on the sandy beach eating crabs.
On the day the aliens came,
I was at the park climbing the tree.
On the day the aliens came
I was watching the sunset.
On the day the aliens came
I was on the mountain reading a book.
On the day the aliens came
I was skiing down a snowy slope.
On the day the aliens came
I was reading How to Tame an Ant.
On the day the aliens came
I was doing Lego in my bedroom.
On the day the aliens came
I was eating strawberry pie.

The Boy on the Green
(Luka Jax, St Martin's.)

Outside a boy is on the green.
It is as dark as a black hole.
In the distance is some light.
It's coming closer and closer and closer.
He's starting to sweat from fear.
It was horrid.
He's only just realised it is a spaceship.
It made him disgusted.
He pulled out his sick gun and vomit went all over it.
It was lime green.
Then they had a party with all of his mates.
It came back and took him to Samoa.
They went snorkelling and saw a grandpa shark and
got to ride it.
He took it to the best theme park,
where there was the busiest and most dangerous
rollercoaster.
They also went to a mountain to hike.
The view at the end was extremely unbelievable!

The Day the Alien Came
(Eva, St Martin's.)

I was in the town centre of Bath
surrounded by a pack of pigeons.
Frogs flooded all over the Circus;
they were all riding cows.
That day, the Circus looked different.
It was an actual circus, filled with fire-breathers and lion tamers.
There was a man covered in pigeons.
My family call him 'Pigeon Paul'.
I was so invested in these events that I didn't notice a beaming light falling closer and closer to the ground.
It landed.
A bright blue UFO stuck to the floor.
A small porthole opened.
One shiny gold head popped out of it.
The alien jumped out.
It was so short. It had a bright purple body,
a hairy tail and bulging fly eyes.
It waddled over to me and waved.
It looked friendly.
'Hello,' I said. 'What planet are you from?'
Although I said this very clearly, I'm not sure it understood English.

‘♏□♓◆♏♒,’

the alien said.
I had no idea what that meant.
I dragged it straight to the library.
We needed to find books to help it learn our language.

Now back to our story:

Chapter 3

The good thing about Jai, the alien, is that he is friendly, and so are we.

So, when he eventually overcame his worries and exited his spaceship that morning, we chatted to him loads and asked him what he would like to do on our planet. Those of us from St Martin's made a list of things we'd like to do with him. After all, he didn't come all this way to sit in our bedrooms playing computer games and chomping crisps.

Here's our list of top ten things:

1) Feed it lots of doughnuts, then chop its head off!
2) Holiday to Samoa.
3) Go to Chuck E. Cheese.
4) Visit the fair.
5) Buy doughnuts and play Roblox.
6) Snorkelling at the beach.
7) Teach it to box professionally.
8) Play Snap!
9) Take it to school and scare the year sixes.
10) Read one of our grandma's TV magazines.

Happily, we're not going to do the first thing on the list because, 1) It's not very nice, and 2) Our stories would be over before we even started.

So, that means that Jai, the alien, is very much alive!

He can't stay for long, so get yourselves ready. Here is what happened when Jai left his grampy behind to repair the spaceship and he got to meet us humans for the first time.

DAY ONE

Day One. Monday.
The one where Ray and Ryver from St Keyna see alien goo!

Today, we took our alien friend, Jai, to school in a flashy vibrant-green Lamborghini. As we pulled up in the car park, Jai had to put on a stealthy disguise so nobody would see his blue and purple torso.

As we stumbled into the classroom, we introduced Jai to the teacher and the children. Suddenly, Jai stuck his arm out and brushed the teacher's wrist. We tried to stop him but it was too late. The teacher turned into a blue and purple alien! All the children screamed as they dashed out of the class.

All of a sudden, there was an explosion, followed by a blazing flickering fire everywhere with smoke filling the whole room. It had anti-alien goo in it and the teacher turned back into a human!

Then we went to breakfast club. We reached the handle, lifted it up and walked in.

Jai picked up the pancakes. We stared at the pancakes for five minutes straight. Green acid rotated around them. The pancakes grew an alien. Our hearts were pounding! Piercing eyes watched us and Jai.

We rushed to the cupboard next to us. Ryver grabbed

the canteen key and unlocked the door. Jai chucked the acid food into the bin full of napkins. Ray clutched the new pancakes and put them on tables one and three.

'What's going on?' shouted a voice behind us. Miss Pain was standing above us.

Ryver explained so fast Miss Pain couldn't understand.

'MY OFFICE NOW! BOTH OF YOU!'

*

(We were going to write more but decided we'd leave the story on a cliffhanger instead. You know, like at the end of a TV show when people freeze and the music goes DA-DA-DAAAAA!)

DAY TWO

Day Two. Tuesday.
The one where Evie V, from St Keyna, sees things upside down.

Me and my alien, Jai, went to a theme park. We took a shiny, white-as-a-marshmallow taxi and talked about all the rides that we'd go on. We also secretly hoped Jai was tall enough for all of them.

When we got there, we saw a loop ride that Jai really wanted to go on. We showed the lady our tickets and ran through to the rollercoaster. No one looked because Jai was wearing a hat and sunglasses as a disguise. At the rollercoaster, Jai had to take them off, so everyone stared and pointed and whispered.

We got on and approached the loop. As we got upside down at the top, it… it…

STOPPED!

Everyone screamed except Jai. He was so used to being upside down because he lived in outer space.

He yelled, 'Don't worry fellow humans! I will call the fire brigade and they will save us.'

They saved us and everyone thanked Jai, and he found out what crowd-surfing was because he did it on the humans.

DAY THREE

Day Three. Wednesday.
The one where Henry from St Keyna takes Jai on holiday.

It was three a.m. in the school holidays. I woke up early because I was going to Spain. Oh yeah, with the alien, Jai! Once we got to the airport, I hid Jai as a lifeguard in a suitcase. I felt nervous but happy as I stepped foot into the plane.

It was bumpy at first, but then it was fine, until… the plane set on fire and started to crash, so Jai got out of the suitcase, and we parachuted into the air.

Next, I found a crystal cave which the engine fell into. So, we landed right next to it. Me and Jai explored but there was a crystal breakdown because all the crystals fell down. We ran away and when it was done, a lava pit and lab were in its place with soldiers guarding the engine. They had weapons so Jai distracted them, and I took the engine and ran but the guard tried to shoot me. I dodged it and got a shield while I ran away with the engine. But then, a massive volcano erupted, and lava and fire were close, so I ran faster.

Finally, we put the engine back in the plane and sprayed water to get rid of the burning fire, and it was majestic and beautiful and we flew away, going past the meteors. In the end, we got to Spain.

ON AIR

DAY FOUR

Day Four. Thursday.

On the fourth day, we thought we'd let Jai have a break from travelling, so some of us from St Michael's set up a special room with chairs and cameras and we interviewed him for our school magazine.

Us: Hello! What's it like coming to Earth?

Jai: *It's a bit strange, but I like it.*

Us: Okay, what's it like trawling around in a spaceship?

Jai: *It's amazing, actually.*

Us: What planet are you from?

Jai: *I'm from a secret star.*

Us: Did you know that when a star is flashing, it's a star, but if it's not then it's a planet?

Jai: *No. But I will note that!*

Us: Why are you here?

Jai: *I was scouting for planets, but also, I heard about Dunkin' Donuts.*

Us: Cool, we'll go get some later. Where did you get your shoes from?

Jai: *I stopped off at a shop on Mars.*

Us: What do you eat?

Jai: *Icyfood.*

Us: Isn't that cold!

Jai: *No. I see food! There! That yellow curvy thing.*

Us: Oh. You want a banana. Here you go!

Jai: *Thank you. Do you have any more questions?*

Us: What language do you speak?

Jai: *Alienese. This is tough!*

Us: You're supposed to take the skin off.

Jai: *Oh. Still nice, though.*

Us: How old are you?

Jai: *42,069,420,694,206,942,069.*

Us: That's very old.

Jai: *I know. But my grampy is five times that.*

Us: Thank you for answering our questions.

Jai: *My pleasure. By the way, did you know if you eat too many of your carrots, you will turn orange?*

Us: It's okay. We don't like carrots.

Interviewed by
Macie, Lacey-Mae, Amelia, Kaci-Mae, Andrew, Whitney and Sonny.

After all those questions, Jai was very tired, and – despite eating four more bananas – extremely hungry, which is why it was very fortunate that Shea from St Keyna arrived to take him back to Keynsham, as she was extremely hungry too.

Me, Isabel, Daren and Jai attached wheels to our hands and feet and drove to McDonald's. We sped through the traffic and threw the wheels off a bridge and sat on air and drove like we were on motorcycles. We ordered McFlurrys, and Gordon Ramsay quit making them because they always splashed around the kitchen, and then the McFlurry machine was out of order, so we hopped over the counter and stole the McFlurry secret formula.

Then we ran out and hopped back on the invisible motorcycles and drove away from Ronald McDonald. We speeded away and Ronald McDonald drove in front of us, so we slammed on our brakes and almost got thrown off. We speeded and duped him, and we all got away with the secret formula.

We may have had the secret formula, but we were the most wanted because people wanted their McFlurrys. So, we made our own ice cream truck and only charged 95p for a McFlurry. Now we're no longer most wanted!

DAY FIVE

Day Five. Friday.
The one where Jai went on holiday once more (this time with Luca and Rhia, Year Four, St Keyna).

Sharks!

At seven-thirty a.m. in Hawaii, Jai and I went to the beach to see the sunrise. It was lucky the lifeguard wasn't there because aliens are not allowed in Hawaii. We took lifeguard clothes and I put them on Jai and we swam together.

Suddenly, we were having so much fun we didn't realise we went too deep in. We just thought it was fine, so we carried on playing and having so much fun.

Oh no! We then saw twenty-one shark fins in the sea. So, we had to swim as fast as we possibly could!

Once we got back to shore on the boiling hot sand, we fell asleep for ten minutes and when we woke up, we realised the sharks were waiting for us to get back in…

TO EAT US!

Then we thought of a plan to catch the sharks. We called 999 for the police to trap them. Once they came, there were fifty helicopters holding the biggest metal cage ever! They dropped the cage on them. We were so happy they were gone!

Chapter 4

All of us were having so much fun with Jai. Wyatt and Rylea (Castle Primary) said making friends with him was like going out into the playground and finding someone on the buddy bench for the first time. They didn't know what to say to him at first but soon ended up having park adventures. They popped into the shop to get their favourite snacks – Takis, Prime and Mr Beast's chocolate bars! They told Jai what they liked about each other – Wyatt liked how one day he left Rylea in the playground, talking to himself. Rylea liked how Wyatt can make him laugh, even when he feels sad.

They promised each other they always will be buddies, even though next year they are going to different secondary schools. Jai loved hearing how humans can become friends.

The rest of us didn't need a buddy bench to chat with Jai, we simply stayed with him in our bedrooms, which was great, except we were all worried that Jai might have to go home soon. Like Evie from Castle Primary was, although she had a hard time hiding him from others!

I sit down on my bed and sigh. I know Jai has to go back at the end of the week, plus I can't keep him hidden any longer. I'm surprised no one has seen him yet.

I look down at him. 'So, how was your week?'

He looks up at me. 'Jai loves it here!'

'I know. We've had lots of fun, but Jai… you need to go back home,' I say. My eyes fill with tears.

Suddenly, I hear footsteps coming up the stairs. I wipe my eyes.

'Someone's coming!' I whisper urgently. I point to the wardrobe and he scampers into it.

The door bursts open.

'Evie! Look at the picture I ma—' My little six-year-old brother, Rowan, stares at me, then at the wardrobe. 'What's in there?'

Rowan came a few seconds too early. Jai's ear is poking out of the wardrobe. He freezes when he hears Rowan's voice.

'Nothing's in there. I like your picture. What is it?' I ask Rowan, hoping he won't ask anything about it.

'It's a penguin, but what's in there?' Rowan gasps. 'Look! It just moved!'

I sigh. There's no point in lying. He'll probably go on about it until I tell him. 'This is Jai. Jai, you can come out!'

Lilie, Millie and Aria from Castle Primary and Daisy from Roundhill School realised it was Jai's last night too.

Jai will have to go home tomorrow. We are going to miss him. We didn't have time to take him to the swimming pool or the stables to ride. But at least we'll watch *Free Rein* on Netflix and eat popcorn and have a sleepover 'til the middle of the night.

'Jai, do you have to go?' Millie asked. 'I'll miss you.'

Jai sat there for a minute.

'Yes. I have to go, but I will come back one day.'

As we peered out the window, the cool summer breeze swirling around us, the pale moonlight gleaming, a whirlwind of emotions gushed through us, overcome by sadness.

'What is it like on the moon?' Lilie asked Jai, while holding hands.

'It is wonderful,' he said kindly.

'Is it made from cheese?'

He smiled and replied, 'No. It's just white rock! But I wish it was!'

We all looked at him. We think he senses our sadness.

'Hey, it's alright!' stammered Jai, attempting to cheer us up. 'Don't dwell on it!'

We snuggled into him, hiding our red puffy eyes from all that crying, sobbing and wailing.

'Aria, come on!' fowned Jai, wiggling his head.

'Yeah!' Aria exclaimed, finally lifting up her head to face him as a tear danced down along her cheek. 'But it's not going to be the same without you!'

And this is the last conversation Natalie from Castle Primary had with him.

'Jai, do you know where's your home? Like, a place where you live?' I asked.

'There.' He reached out his pale arms, a delicate finger pointing at a minute, distant star.

I took out my handy camera – ideally sized for my pocket – focusing onto his figure.

'What are you taking pictures of? The night sky?' he asked with a childish tone, giving me a radiant smile far too big for his face.

'Nothing really. Just something precious.'

That evening, everything changed.

'Hey, can I talk to you for a bit?' he enquired. 'I… it's against my nature to continue dwelling in your home, so…'

I was dumbed still. Eyes wide. Sat frozen. 'W-what do you mean? You're leaving?' I practically yelled the words at him.

He jumped backwards in shock, leaning towards the left side of my room as he avoided my gaze.

'Look. I know you are upset, but, like… I… I need to go home.' His voice was desperate and pleading.

Awkward silence. Only the faint tick, tick, tick of my alarm clock.

'So… what are your plans when you return home?' That's when I realised how dazed he suddenly looked, like someone seeing sunlight after spending a lifetime in darkness.

'Well, expanding my planet would be nice, and maybe planting flowers as well, because they remind me of you.' He looked at the time.

Nine-thirty.

'I'll miss you so much, honestly,' I said. 'Promise to visit me, please.'

'Promise.'

I shook his hand. It was cold and fragile.

I told him I'd keep a picture of him, with a cheap Post-it-note on it, and in black Sharpie ink, I scribbled – Jai.

Chapter 5

Jai's grampy couldn't fix the spaceship, but one of our dads was a mechanic and he discovered the engine fault was down to a broken connection between the instrument panel and the main thrusters.

Jai had only been with us on Earth for seven days, but that was light years on his planet. He had family he wanted to go back to – his mum, his dad, his brother, Igi, and his flazzzoo, Haggy, who he described as being a bit like the cats we have on Earth.

Isabelle from Roundhill School walked him back to his spaceship.

We had tears in our eyes but all the while we were hoping we'd all meet again. Jai walked up the gangplank to the spaceship and held Grampy's hand. The machine door closed and the warm engine rumbled like a lion's stomach waiting for food. And we all stood and watched as the spaceship lifted off the ground, then hovered above us in the sky. Some of us shouted, 'Goodbye'. Others shouted, 'We love you!' and we saw Jai smiling at the window, waving his hand.

'I won't forget you!' we all think he said.

And then he was gone, zooming through the clouds.

We stood and looked at each other.

We would all miss him. We hoped he knew.

'Let's write him letters,' someone shouted.

'And poems!'

'Yeah!'

'Yeah!'

'But where do we send them?'

'Easy,' someone else said. 'We'll just address them, *Dear Jai, somewhere beyond the moon.*'

Malakai McCabe,
Year Six, Roundhill School,
sent him this:

Goodbye Alien

The last seven days were amazing, but I'm sad you have to leave!

I'll walk you to your spaceship and we'll talk about this week!

On Monday, we went to the zoo and became the animals!

Tuesday, we went to my room and turned it into a cool car!

Wednesday, we went to space and flew to the moon!

Thursday, we went to my school and hid from the teachers!

Friday, we went to KFC and ordered the whole menu!

Saturday, we went to an ice-cream shop and got one-hundred scoops!

And now it is Sunday, and we need to take you home,
but first, let's fly around the world!
Go to the bottom of the sea!
Dance to music and drink a cup of tea!
Remember what we did this week
and then we'll go to my school,
where Stewart – the author – will be!
Then we'll say goodbye and see you another day,
but you'll come back soon and we'll do it all again!
Monday, Tuesday, Wednesday – we can be here on Earth!
Thursday, Friday, Saturday – we can be at my hearth!
Sunday, I'll go home and will remember the time you spent here.
Goodbye, alien, see you on another adventure!

Tyler-Jay Gillard, Year Six, Roundhill School, sent this.

The Space in Spaceship

I was so sad the day you left me.

We saw the ducks chasing the greedy birds because they robbed their food we gave out. You once said if you take away the space in spaceship it will float on water.

I thought that was clever.

You said your name was Jai because your brother was an AI.

I thought that was funny.

We went to the shop for picnic supplies, but it seemed closed because everyone was scared of you.

I wish you'd come back or I could see your planet or house. You said it's made of cheese as a joke. You made me laugh when you pretended to be a pizza man that I didn't order. That was how we became best friends.

It's sad when you need a new friend and when you get one, they leave you so early.

Last time I ate food with you, we had a food fight in an empty field behind my house surrounded by trees. We even tried to play football like we were in the FC finals and I won against you.

I hope life changes back, Jai, so I can see you again, and see you walk back to me instead of walking away, back to your home.

Everyone wanted to send some space mail!

SPACE
MAIL

Anna Jobil,
Year Six, Roundhill School.

A Letter to Jai

Jai,

I loved it when you came to visit. I remember when we went to the beach and collected seashells and built sandcastles. A crab pinched your nose.

When we went to the park and you fell off the seesaw.

When we went to a swimming pool and you fell off the slide.

I miss you so much. You were so much fun to play with and I was devastated when you left. We used to buy chocolate doughnuts, triple chocolate fudge, chocolate cake and double chocolate brownies.

Goodbye, and I hope you will visit me!

P.S: I remember when you helped the boy who laughed at you when he fell off his scooter. You taught me to be kind to everyone.

SCARY

Efron Aneesh, Year Six,
Roundhill School.

I miss…

I really miss you, Jai.
I enjoyed spending time with you.
I miss going to the park at midnight and you
jump-scaring me.
I miss telling you ghost stories and scaring you.
I miss playing hide and seek with strangers who didn't
even know they were playing.
I still remember going to the beach and scaring you
with creatures I didn't even know the name of.
I also remember me and you almost getting caught on
camera, so yeah. That was close.
I still look up at the sky, hoping you'll come back.
I wish we had longer.

Aaron Saji, Year Six, Roundhill School.

The Good Times

The day you left, I asked why you had to go. You said your grampy cannot stay here forever. He wanted to see his wife. He didn't like the food and is so old and getting older fast on Earth.

As I walked you to the spaceship, I remembered the good times: eating ice cream, playing Roblox together, snowball fights, climbing trees, making my room zero gravity, playing football, scaring my human friends, eating chocolate, making a pet robot, learning maths, making paintings, meeting my mum and dad, going to the beach, teaching you to read and write English, reading *Beast Quest Epos vs Ferno*; and the important thing: when we met near the bus stop near Whiteway Road where I live and I asked you where you were going at first, but you were too shy to speak up and you said, 'Bee Bee Boo Boo Baa Baa.' (I didn't know what you were saying). I bought an AirPod that could do something cool: if I spoke English, you would hear my voice in your language. I gave you one and I had one and now I am quite sad that you left for home. I didn't speak to anyone for a few days after you left planet Earth, but I told everyone about my alien friend and all the good old times we had.

Chapter 6

We realise that reading those letters might make you feel a little sad, but that's what happens when you miss something or someone, bad. But there is a happy end to this story, because after Jai left, we all agreed that every night we would take it in turns to watch the sky, just in case he decided to come back, or send us all a message.

And one night, he did. With bright penlight, zapping across the sky. Amy Harris in Keynsham saw it first, and she shouted across the road to James King, and he's got such a big voice that everyone in his street heard it – then his whole housing estate. It was so loud it reached us all in Bath.

We all ran outside and looked up. The bright penlight was now zapping from star to star, like it was joining them up.

'What's happening,' one of us shouted.

'It's Jai,' said someone else. 'I think he's writing us a message in the sky.'

We all felt ourselves smiling as Jai drew letters that formed into words.

Hey everyone. I read your messages. I love and miss you all too! And just so you know, I had an amazing time with you on Earth. I loved all the things I did with you, and all the conversations we had. And hey, Seb from St Mary's, I will always remember the poem you wrote about us being in a band.

My Band

There are aliens in town.
When they arrived,
they descended down.
I was alone,
but I made a friend.
We stole a car
and went round the bend.
We became best friends
and formed a band.
We went to the beach and played in the sand.

Goodbye, everyone, I really hope, hope, hope, that I come back to Earth soon.

THE DAY THE
ALIEN
CAME

And that is the end of our story. We hope you enjoyed it because we had lots of fun writing about that amazing day, when Jai, the alien, came to Earth. But we aren't quite finished yet. Because even though we didn't have enough pages for all of us to tell our stories, these pieces were just tooooo good, not to be in it.

Kara, Year Five, St Mary's.

It was evening, and the sun was descending as the moon rose, sparkling proudly. A sudden beeping noise echoed through the air. My window gave me a feeling that something was watching me, which gave me goosebumps just thinking about it."

Baylee, Year Five, St Mary's.

Before time, I was in the Viking ages. I sit in the snow watching a man fight the monsters, defending our village. Suddenly, I feel a change in the breeze. I see a circle in the sky. It looks like it's gonna crash.

Poppy, Year Five, St Mary's.

There are smells like toffee apples and toxic waste.

Idhika, St Martin's.

I am in the dark night looking at the moon. I see an aeroplane on the stormy sky.

Rudy and Faith, Year Five, St Mary's.

He sees there is a puppy party and there are puppies singing and stage diving. The puppies carry the alien to the stage. The alien joins the acrobatics and does a backflip and so do the puppies.

Harmiony, St Martin's.

On a dark gloomy night on the beach, I can hear a cloud storm…

Ava-Rose, Year Five, St Mary's.

Puppy parties are the best, that's when the alien came to town. Yummy food was all around.

Puppy parties are the best, after we get our best party dress.

Efa, Year Five, St Mary's.

I was in my house and something was in the distance from the window. It was a creepy spaceship from up above, but it crashed into our roof! I asked myself if it was actually an alien. I checked it out and the spaceship opened up and I was worried.

Tommy, Year Five, St Mary's.

We went through multiple galaxies and landed on planet Dong Bong Bing Ding Bob. It was made of sweets with lots of animals that are friendly, and on the other side there is a Shrek army with gremlins and a beast. Well, that's what the sign said.

Harry Archer Miles, St Martin's.

I see a big scary man in the park, chasing me. Next to me I see a UFO as I run. It gets closer. I feel sick. It sounds like a beeping truck reversing backwards. I smell petrol leaking out.

Mason Spurrey, Year Five, St Martin's.

It was black, dark and I saw the vague outline of a person walking towards me whilst breathing heavily. It was scary, gloomy and terrifying.

Charlie White, Year Five, St Martin's.

It was a dark night and I was at the top of a mountain, looking up in the sky.

Valarian, Year Five, St Martin's.

Something was wrong. It was diving towards me. It made a roaring sound as it screamed through the air.

Conan, Year Five, St Martin's.

I was in a box and saw a UFO drop an out-of-date cheeseburger.

George Archer Miles, St Martin's.

Late at night, I saw a massive thing in the sky. I could not tell what it was, but it was terror. I heard a super loud buzzing sound. I saw a disgusting green thing in the sky which had blood all over it, I think, and each day it got closer to me I was terrified. It came into my house, but it only wanted to play with me, so we went to a theme park. We went bowling after, and both got two strikes, and also had loads of pizzas. We had a fantastic time, and after the day was over, we never saw each other again.

Derric Niggeah, St Martin's.

I see a suspicious alien in the UFO. It was staring at me. I was in the spa. I hear a cracking noise from the clouds. To his astonishment, I saw a spiteful sternly nose in the red blood moon. I felt rumbling because an earthquake was hitting in the outer core.

Yesenia Oakes, Year Six,
Roundhill School.

I miss the alien's silly, droopy antennae. I felt upset and lonely without their presence. I saw his funny face draw away into the sky in his ship. I will always remember.

Charlie Fry, Year Six,
Roundhill School.

I was so very sad when I saw my friend walking away forever. I remember seeing his eyes filled with tears and so were mine as I watched from my room. But I still have happy times, like the day we had ice cream, you dropped yours so we shared my one. You are the best alien a boy could ask for. I hope I see you very soon, my friend.

Myah Thomas, Year Six,
Roundhill School.

I loved how we went to the rainy beach and got soaked like swans in the cold water.

A peek inside the Flying Saucer

Cabin pressure regulator
Boost circuit
Photon accumulator
Warp generator

Phoebe Robson, Year Six, Roundhill School.

I was feeling sad that I was never going to see the alien again. I wrote down everything we did in the past week. We have been getting free food because the people who work in the shops run outside in fright. It really is funny seeing everyone run away because of Jai. He is my best friend and isn't scary at all.

Molly Shearn, Year Six, Roundhill School.

I will extremely miss the amazing times we had together, like the time Jai went to the Roman Baths and swam in the water, then got kicked out!

Joe, Year Six, St Martin's.

I was in Bath, all alone on a foggy day with nothing to do. The wind was howling like a wolf, when the sky turned black, filled with fuel.

Samir, Year Six, St Martin's.

I was driving around with my family on the way to Vicky Park when I saw an alien spaceship land on the grass at the Circus. As I saw it land, we rushed to the place. The alien started talking to me as I jumped out of the car. My heart thumped with excitement!

Brooke-Lynn, Year Six, St Martin's.

I was in my front garden and heard a buzzing sound coming from the sky. 'Vmmm!' it went. I was confused! I thought it was coming from a lawn mower, but I was wrong. All of a sudden, flashing lights appeared from the sky. 'Beep, beep, beep!' They got brighter by the second. I saw a UFO! I was flabbergasted. It landed and I sprinted across and knocked on it. 'Tut, tut, tut!' The doors slid open.

Harvey, Year Six, St Martin's.

I was playing *Pokémon GO*, walking on the Linear park (I'd just evolved a Doduo) but while I was about to exit the first tunnel, an alien came down in a salami-shaped flying saucer!

'I have searched the universe for someone that I can actually beat in *Pokémon GO*,' said the alien.

While the alien was talking, I snuck on his ship and grabbed his teleporter.

'... And furthermore... wait— what are you doing with my teleporter?' asked the alien in shock.

'Getting help!' I replied as I teleported Rory and Arthur to my location. 'RAID BATTLE!'

Cemre, Year Six, St Martin's.

I laughed. I thought it was a costume, but the alien was leaving sticky marks on the bench he was sitting on. I was afraid. I wanted to ask all the questions in my mind, but just as I was about to gather all my self-confidence and leave, he got up and was walking with a notebook in his hand. He looked at me.

Michelle, Year Six, St Martin's.

I was taking a drink from downstairs when I saw something glowing. I was curious, so I went out and hid in a bush to see what was going on. After a minute, a spaceship landed and an alien walked out of it!

The following pages showcase some of the wonderful drawings produced by the children during the process of writing this book.

by Andrew Shell

Acknowledgements

Thank you to Toni and Tim Warren for their guidance and support of this project.

This project would not have been possible without the generous support of our sponsors.

Headline Sponsors:

Thank you to Almeda Facilities, The Curated Property Company, Evelyn Partners and Thrings Solicitors for your contributions as our headline sponsors.

Silver Sponsors:

We extend our gratitude to Cazenove Capital and YTL Utilities UK for your support as silver sponsors.

Bronze Sponsors:

Thank you to Buro Happold, Carter Jonas and F&S Building Contractors for your support as bronze sponsors.

The sponsorship of these organisations has been crucial in helping us bring the children's stories to life.

About this project

In 2024, St John's is turning 850 years old. To celebrate this milestone anniversary we embarked on a special project that harnessed the creative minds of 192 primary pupils from seven local schools in Bath and North East Somerset.

The children featured within these pages are now published authors, and it is their hard work, imagination and enthusiasm that have brought this magical story to life. Through this project, we aim to highlight the incredible power of reading and literature. We hope that each child involved will forever cherish the memory of writing this book, inspiring them to continue exploring the world through words.

Find out more about the work St John's does to ensure every child has the best start in life on our website:

stjohnsbath.org.uk/what-we-do/supporting-children/

About the author
Stewart Foster

When I was ten years old, there was a writing competition at school. For three weeks I wrote what felt like every evening and handed my story in. Three exercise books filled with my scruffy writing, scared I'd done it wrong because everyone in my class had completed two pages at most.

Come the presentation assembly, my deafness meant I had to ask my sister, in Year Four, to tell me the outcome. As the headteacher stood on the stage, all I could hear was muffled syllables, then three hundred children turning, my sister pointing at me – but I refused to move. Until my class teacher, Mr Grimshaw, tapped me on the shoulder and whispered, 'Stew, you've won!' The prize was to have my book, 'published' and placed in the school library for all to read.

That school was Twerton's St Michael's, a half mile-walk down the hill from my infant school, and a ten-minute run from the house in Freeview Road where I grew up.

Many years on and a few more published books later, St John's Foundation asked me to go back to the area and visit the seven schools within their Best Start in Life initiative. I had no idea what an amazing experience I was about to have with the children, and certainly no indication of the incredible work we would produce.

So, what you are holding in your hands right now, is their book. The result of my visits, guidance, but ultimately their hard work and imagination. There are lines that will make you laugh, poems that will make you cry, because when an alien lands its spaceship near your school, that's the sort of emotions it can bring out.

This project has been an absolute blast from beginning to end and I'm hugely grateful to St John's for the faith they put in me, to the teachers who engaged and joined us all on this journey. I also owe a huge debt to my daughter, Lois, who, whilst I went from school to school having fun, stayed glued to her laptop, collating the two hundred pieces of writing I sent her.

But the biggest praise has to go to the children, who welcomed me into their classroom and lives, who laughed at my bad jokes, listened intently to the stories, and jumped at the chance to become part of Jai, the alien's story. This is a final message to them: yes, we all worked hard, did the boring bits where we had to check our spelling and punctuation, but boy, we did have the most brilliant fun.

Stewart Foster is the author of one novel for adults, *We Used to Be Kings* and children's novels *The Bubble Boy, All The Things That Could Go Wrong, Check Mates* and many others.

About the illustrator
Andrew Prescott

I have loved drawing and painting for as long as I can remember and have worked in the creative industry since graduating from art college.

Working on *The Day The Alien Came* has been a real pleasure and the inspiration behind all the illustrations is from the incredible imaginations of the children involved in the project.

I have designed and illustrated many books over the years on a broad range of topics and it's been fun creating amazing characters, including dogs, cats, monsters, dragons, wizards and even a sheep called Merlin! Now I can add space aliens to my repertoire.